DATE DUE			

THE MAGIC DISK

ISBN 0-89868-490-0–Library Bound
ISBN 0-89868-491-9–Soft Bound
ISBN 0-89868-492-7-Trade

A PREDICTABLE WORD BOOK

THE
MAGIC DISK

Story by Janie Spaht Gill, Ph.D.
Illustrations by Gerald Rogers

 ARO PUBLISHING

One day John was playing with a computer inside his house.

He put in a new disk and then clicked down on the mouse.

4

5

On the screen appeared
the words, "I will give you
3 wishes of your choosing
before the day is through."

John thought of Basketball
And how he never scored at all.

Inside the room, suddenly there was a great, "poof!" John grew and grew, then suddenly, his head shot through the roof!

11

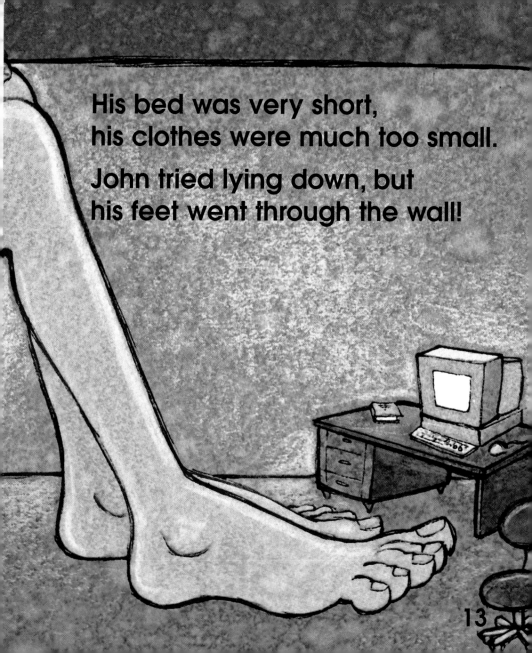

His bed was very short,
his clothes were much too small.

John tried lying down, but
his feet went through the wall!

13

When friends came to the door
what they saw were legs and feet.

They screamed and ran in fear,
causing chaos in the streets.

"I hate being tall," said John.
"I wish that I were small."

Then with a great "poof,"
he was hard to see at all.

17

His clothes were much too big.
His bed was much too high.

Looking up at the bedposts
looked like a tower in the sky.

"I wish this hadn't happened," said John, "being small is such a pain."

Then with one great, "poof," John was normal size again.

21